WILD

MATING SEASON

ELIZA GAYLE

GYPSY INK BOOKS

GET THE NEWS

Make sure you sign up for my newsletter at elizagayle. com/newsletter for all the up-to-date book news, FREE books, and my complimentary grimoire of behind the scenes goodies.

PRO TIP: Make sure you add eliza@elizagayle.com to your contacts list to ensure the newsletter goes straight to your inbox.

DEVILS POINT WOLVES

WILD

by Eliza Gayle

Published by Gypsy Ink Books, © 2015 Eliza Gayle

eliza@elizagayle.com
http://ElizaGayle.com
Eliza on Instagram
Eliza on Facebook
Eliza on Goodreads

Book Description:

Mating Season is in full swing and she has no idea what she's walking into.

Faith is on the cusp of having it all.

She made it through the last of her college finals and is looking forward to starting her career. If only her twin would answer her damned phone.

After three days of no word, she's forced to drive to Devils Point and search for her. As her luck goes, things go south the minute she hits creepy island.

Starting with a wolf attack that lands her in hot water with her sister's boss.

Damien just wants to get through Mating Season and get back to normal.

His would be mate is not at all what he expected and not exactly his type. Not to mention off limits. Until she shows up smelling like another wolf.

Now all bets are off and he'll do anything to protect her--including claim her.

Faith Harris stared down the unlit two lane road that would take her across the bay to Devils Point. The creepiest place on earth and current home of her insane twin sister.

Maybe she wasn't clinically insane, but there had to be something going wrong in that brain of hers to move out here in what felt like the middle of nowhere despite being in relative close proximity to a city the size of Tacoma.

The Pacific Northwest had a lot going for it with fresh air and lots of mountains and water, but these foggy islands were really not her thing. She preferred the creature comforts that came with living in Seattle just an hour or so away.

Restaurants galore, a coffee shop on every corner to feed her caffeine addiction, and a safe, secure apartment building only a few blocks away from the college campus.

When she reached the bridge and looked over the water she saw nothing. The low lying white fog had rolled in and reduced visibility to barely a few feet in front of her car.

Faith continued slowly, hoping against hope that if any other cars were on the bridge with her, that they would stay the heck on their side of the road.

As soon as she found her sister, Rebel and was assured she was not dead lying in a ditch somewhere, she was going to kill her.

Kill her.

Ever since the death of their parents four years ago, she'd been forced to become the mother figure to her minutes younger sister whether she liked it or not. Unfortunately, with a name like Rebel, her twin did everything she could to live up to her name and then some.

And like her name, she was the polar opposite. Faith the good girl.

Just thinking it made her cringe. Did anyone ever stop to consider maybe she didn't want to be the angel sister? Maybe she wanted to get a job in a strip club literally called Club Diablo on a creepy, foggy island and meet man after man without a care in the world.

She laughed. It was the most absurd thought she'd had to date. Unlike Rebel, she tried everything to hide her curvy body instead of flaunt it. Even the few times she had sex, she did everything she could to keep the lights off.

So yeah, stripping had to be her dumbest thought. And lately these crazy thoughts were hitting her on a too frequent basis. Not that it surprised her. Her stress levels had gone through the roof as she went through the last of her finals and the fact her sister was not answering any of her calls didn't help.

Faith frowned. This is exactly why she drove to this God forsaken island in the first place. So she could give Rebel a piece of her mind in person. She only hoped it ended up as another false alarm and she'd find her sister shacked up with some new guy screwing like rabbits.

Before her mind could spiral out of control with worry once again, something moved in her peripheral vision. Automatically her head jerked to the right and saw nothing but fog. A chill ran up her spine as she turned to face the road again only to find a giant animal in the road directly in her path.

She white knuckled the steering wheel and slammed on the brakes, hoping to God they didn't lock up before she got the car stopped. But the road was wet and the animal a little too close. Her brakes squealed and the scent of burning rubber hit her hard as her car screamed to a stop with a last minute thud as she struck something with her front tire.

She slowly peeled her numb fingers from the wheel and with one hand quickly shoved the gear into park. The rest of her body shook as equal parts fear and adrenaline coursed through her.

That animal had shown up in the road out of nowhere in a matter of seconds. What the heck was it anyway? A really big dog? Maybe a deer? She strained to see something—anything through the fog, but after a few moments collapsed against the seat in frustration.

She was going to have to get out and look. Her stomach lurched. The idea of finding one of God's beautiful creatures had become road kill because her reflexes weren't fast enough made her sick.

Why in hell had she driven all the way out here after dark? She could have waited until morning to come.

Because she had a bad feeling and she couldn't shake it, that's why.

With only one option to discover what happened, Faith unbuckled her seat belt and turned on her hazard lights before easing from the car. The one and only indulgence she allowed herself in the last four and a half years was the dark green mini cooper that she splurged on with money she saved and scrimped on from multiple jobs and a little of the life insurance money left to her from her parents.

Her steps dragged as she made her way around the front end and looked down at the road. And found nothing. What the hell?

She walked around the entire length of the car and squatted by the hood and searched underneath with no results. Relieved that she hadn't killed whatever animal that had appeared in the road, she blew out a hard breath and pushed her hand through her long hair.

A quick glance over her car didn't reveal any damage to her mini either. *Thank God.* Although she'd have to wait until morning to be sure. Visibility sucked out here.

A loud snap from behind made her jump. She whirled around and found a wolf not ten feet from her. Not just a wolf, this thing was massive. It probably stood to her waist. With her heart beating wildly, she took several steps back.

She glanced at her car realizing the path to her door was now blocked by a creature whose lips were now curled up, baring his teeth.

Now what?

She could run, but her every instinct told her if she did it would only encourage an attack. Didn't animals like to chase their prey?

"Hey there, sweet doggie," she cooed with a shaky voice. "I didn't mean to hit you. I didn't see you. Are you okay?" She kept her tone light hoping that he'd sense she meant no harm.

He growled in response and took a few steps closer. Faith backed up until her hip hit the corner of her car. There really was no other choice at this point than to run.

She turned on her heel and headed around the car and sprinted toward the woods. As she feared, she probably got less than a hundred feet before she felt the wolf at her back pushing her with his big front paws into the dirt face first.

Tears burned at her eyes as she rolled, wriggling free from the legs pressing down on her back.

"I am not about to die at the hands of some mangy wolf." She bared her own teeth in defense. "I have a sister that needs me to take care of her."

The wolf stared at her and for a moment she'd almost swear it understood her. His head cocked to the side and his eyes focused in on her. For a few seconds she got her hopes up there might be a way out of this.

Then he bared his teeth again and dove at her. This time his mouth locked on her wrist and its teeth dug through her flesh. Faith screamed and fought with her free hand, digging her fingers into the animal's neck. Pain streaked up her arm as she fought for her life. She even lifted her leg and tried to kick the wolf in the backside. But nothing shook him free of the hold he now had on her arm.

"Help!" she screamed, knowing full well no one was out here to bother with her.

To her surprise a loud bang came from somewhere deep inside the fog. The wolf flinched and his mouth popped open, releasing her arm.

Faith had no idea what was going on but she didn't care. She spun around and raced around the back end of her car and jumped inside, hitting the lock button as soon as it closed. She tried to twist the keys and get the engine started but her hands shook uncontrollably.

"Shit. Fuck. Damn." Tears streamed down her face as fear consumed her. She had no idea where the wolf was or where that mysterious shot came from. At least she assumed it was a gun shot. Nothing else made sense.

"Calm down and breath. As long as I stay in the car, he can't get to me," she told herself.

Her heart raced, beating so damn hard her chest ached. But she managed to take a deep breath and blow it out slowly, giving her just enough focus to turn the keys. To her surprise ,the engine started immediately and she wasted no time throwing it into gear and stomping her foot on the gas as hard as she could.

The car lurched forward and shot into the fog, visibility be damned. She no longer cared what she hit or what might pop out of the dense moisture. The bar where her sister worked wasn't far past the bridge and she only had to get there before anyone shot at her again.

D amien peered through the smoke filled room to the woman standing just inside the door. Long blonde hair nearly to her ass, pale porcelain skin, curvy compact body, and without seeing them, crystal blue eyes.

They weren't hard to imagine when every time he closed his eyes they haunted him. As did everything about her.

Her curves alone were enough to drive a man wild...

Faith Harris, the thorn in his side, the woman of his dreams and a fragile human who had no idea what he really was, had stepped into his bar uninvited. Looked like his night was about to go sideways.

At the moment he was plotting his escape, she spotted him at the bar and with a subtle fling of her silky hair, she headed his way. She wasn't the type to flaunt her body, but each step she took in his direction teased him mercilessly. His body tightened the closer she got and he had to adjust himself to save his poor manhood.

As the sister to one of his employees, he'd only met her a couple of times, so his immediate and undeniable reaction frustrated him. Although in his defense there had also been more than a few phone calls where he'd spoken to her since she did check up on her sister all the damn time. Each one of those instances had left him aching to go after her.

Unfortunately for him, he could smell the innocence on her and he wanted no part of that. He preferred his women more experienced and with low expectations no matter how good they smelled.

He wasn't the settling down type, and the last thing he wanted to do was lead her on--or hurt her.

Of course she'd arrive in the throes of mating season when it made good choices a lot harder when it came to the ladies. Especially ripe-for-the-picking human ones with a mother figure complex. It made her a perfect candidate to bear pack pups.

Just then his nose caught a different scent and the wolf inside him went on high alert. The sweet coppery smell of blood filled his head and the closer Faith got to him the stronger it got. Was she injured? Had someone dared to hurt her?

With his anger swiftly rising, this time he looked closer, beyond his memories and his sense of smell. There was a smudge of dirt on her face and what looked like leaves scattered through her hair. But it was the bare arm with a bandage wrapped around her wrist that made him growl.

"Easy brother. You're going to scare her away if you jump her now."

Diego, his brother and one of the three co owners of Club Diablo with him, eased behind the bar next to him.

"She's hurt."

"Yes, she is. That's what I came to talk to you about. Dante found her outside sobbing in her car. She was scared witless and terrified to step outside. He calmed her down, but we have a problem."

He jerked, turning to his brother. "What happened? Tell me quick."

A small smile quirked at the edges of Diego's mouth before he turned serious again. "Says she was attacked by an abnormally large wolf out on the bridge. Apparently, she thought she hit him with her car and when she got out to investigate, he attacked her."

The wolf inside Damien pushed at his control. He wanted out and he wanted out right now. The beast would avenge her. "Who?" he asked.

"Don't know yet. Doesn't smell familiar at all. Definitely shifter though."

He didn't like the sound of that. "Rogue? Here on the island?"

Diego nodded. "Appears so. Just what we need right now."

"No shit." He turned back around and watched Faith wind her way through the crowd. Her usually pale skin looked even more pale and he detected a slight tremble at her lower lip. Her fear washed over him and caused his stomach to tighten. She had no business being in here right now. Not with this randy crowd.

As of the new moon, Club Diablo had temporarily changed over to a different clientele for mating season. Instead of the usual female dancers, this week they had all male dancers, which drew in a lot of women from neighboring towns and every non-mated wolf within scenting distance came in right behind them.

Which meant the club was an overload of pheremones at the moment and Faith's fear wasn't going to be much of a deterrent.

"We need to get her the hell out of here," Damien said, gaze still glued on the approaching woman. Each lush inch of her pulling at his wolf as well as the man. At least what he could see of her.

He had no idea why she hid her lush figure under baggy clothes making it almost impossible for him to track the curve of her hips or the swell of her high and full breasts.

Although for once he was grateful. Diablo clientele had plenty of flesh to ogle at the moment between the men on the stage and the over active women vying for attention in the crowd.

"Where's my sister?" Faith stopped in front of him, keeping a comfortable distance between them when she did. It struck him that her strong instincts told her he wasn't someone to trifle with. And yet when she opened her mouth...

Damien raised his brow, amused by her demanding tone. "You're hurt." He ignored her question and nodded toward the bandage at her wrist.

She quickly swung her arm behind her back. "I'm fine. It's my sister I'm worried about. She hasn't returned any of my calls in days. So where is she?"

"Rebel has the night off. As you can see we've got a different group of dancers in."

Faith turned her head and curled her lip at the men and women near the stage. "So I see."

"You don't approve?" He couldn't resist the question. For some reason he couldn't pass up an opportunity into goading this woman. Considering how much her mere presence taunted him it only seemed fair.

She shrugged. "Doesn't matter whether I approve or not. People do what people do. It's human nature."

He swallowed a laugh. She might think she knew about human nature from her studies in Forensic Science and Sociology at the University of Washington, but she had no idea what really lurked in the world. At least not yet. It seemed his young temptress was headed for a rude awakening in the worst way.

"Did you try the motel? If anyone knows where she is I'd bet Mavis or Bud would have the answer. She stays with them."

Faith jerked her gaze from the stage and focused her big blue eyes directly on him. "I came here first. It was closest. Plus I assumed my sister would be working tonight. She loves to dance."

The scent of fear surrounding Faith deepened. Damien reached out and covered her hand, fighting the need to pull her tight against him so that he could feel her heart beat against his skin. She didn't know it yet, but the wolf inside him would kill to protect her. "You're scared. Tell me why?" He needed to hear the story in her own words.

She pulled her hand free and shifted her gaze toward the floor. "It doesn't matter anymore. It's over. Now I just need to find my sister so I can go home. This place freaks me out."

Again her instincts were spot on. "Then I will take you to the motel and together we will find her." Rebel was probably sleeping off her bender. Dante had reported in on her earlier and mentioned a half empty bottle of Tequila. She was not taking the news about shifters and mating season very well at all. And if she couldn't cope with it, how in the hell would this one?

"It would be great to find her tonight. The sooner I do, the sooner I can get away from here."

She was definitely scared. He hated that he was going to be the one to break the news of her current predicament. Specifically, that she wouldn't be leaving the island anytime soon.

CHAPTER
THREE

Faith didn't want to look at Damien right now. The attack had left her feeling vulnerable and the strange way he treated her left her even more unsettled. One minute he looked at her like she was something special and the next like something he couldn't get off his shoe. The mixed signals from him drove her nuts on a good day. Today? She couldn't handle it.

Right now all she could think about was being back in the safety of her secure apartment building where there was no reason for her to drive through fog and certainly no wild animals to run in front of her car and then attack her when she tried to help them.

Except getting back to said apartment involved climbing back in her car and returning the way she came. As far as she knew there was only one way on or off this stupid island.

When she didn't say anything else, Damien frowned. "Come with me," he said as he turned, and walked toward the door. She got the distinct impression he just assumed she'd follow him.

Every bone in her body wanted to stay put and not follow him anywhere, but her worry for her sister took precedence over her trivial discomfort.

She grabbed her wrist and rubbed it a few times, trying to dull the burning pain that continued to flare up around her wound. The first thing she needed to do when she got back to the mainland would be rabies shots. No telling what kind of diseases these wild animals carried around.

Damien led her out of the bar and directly to a big, black SUV with dark tinted windows that loomed in front of her. A Hummer in fact that had to be three times the size of her little car. He held the door open for her and even offered her a hand climbing in.

"I'm surprised you don't have a ladder to get into this thing. We could just take my car."

"I need a vehicle that I actually fit inside. Unlike that thing." He purposely pointed to her mini knowing full well it belonged to her.

He was probably right. Of course his reference to his size inevitably led her brain down an entirely different path. He was the first man she'd ever met who actually made her feel like a small sized woman. As she buckled her belt she watched him walk around the car, admiring every step he took.

They didn't make men like him and his two brothers in Seattle that's for sure. At six foot something (a lot of something for sure), broad shoulders, narrow hips and thick thighs, currently encased in black pants obviously tailored to fit him like a glove, he was certainly a sight to behold. And if that wasn't enough there was the rest of him. Thick, dark hair he kept combed back from his face, chiseled jaw covered with enough hair to be sexy but not so much to be lumberjacky. Even his bushy eyebrows looked sexy where on anyone else they would make her think unibrow.

She didn't even want to get started on the green eyes she currently couldn't see. Not when she couldn't tear her eyes off the shape of his ass as he walked in front of the vehicle. Jesus. What was wrong with her? She was acting like some sort of sex starved idiot.

Well...

Maybe she wasn't exactly starving but she certainly had a nice dry spell going when it came to all things sex. Because who had time for that when school consumed ninety-eight percent of her time and the other two percent were taken up with things like sleep, food and sister troubles?

When they reached the small downtown area she looked around marveling how adorable it seemed. There was a small coffeeshop/bakery sandwiched between an auto mechanic shop and a tiny police station with honey buns in the window that made her mouth water, reminding her she'd forgotten to eat both lunch and dinner today.

She stared an unmarked building that kind of looked like it might be an apartment building based on the balconies at each unit. Some of them held portable grills while others were teeming with plants. Why hadn't Rebel moved into one of those instead of insisting on the local motel as a more comfortable choice?

As they moved beyond the apartments, they passed a teeny tiny library that also seemed to serve as some sort of town hall according to the signs outside.

At the very end of the main drive sat the one and only motel that served the island and was little more than a row of rooms and a blinking soda machine sitting outside the front office.

Damien pulled into the lot and parked in front of the room marked #7, coincidentally her sister's favorite number. Rebel put faith in all things odd and had a real thing about making your own luck by following her little rituals.

There were no cars parked out front and she wasn't sure whether that was a good sign or not. Her sister didn't have a car at the moment after selling her last one. Claimed she didn't need one here on the island and said her boss let her borrow one if she needed to go off island.

As soon as Damien got the car parked, Faith opened the door and jumped down, ignoring the pain shooting up her arm. She ran to the door and knocked while trying the knob at the same time only to discover the darn thing locked.

"Rebel, open up. It's me." She waited a few heart beats hoping her sister would answer her before knocking again. This time she put her ear to the door and listened. She heard something... Was that snoring?

"I think I hear her." She banged harder on the door and yelled. "Rebel, open the door already!"

Damien looked a little annoyed standing next to her, which must have gotten old quick as he walked to the office and disappeared inside. Moments later he reappeared and held up a key.

"They just gave you a key?"

"Of course. Everyone knows everyone on this island. In fact, Billy said he saw her a few hours ago all alone and drunk as a skunk. His words by the way. He thinks she's probably sleeping it off by now."

This news did not comfort her at all. Rebel had a wild streak a mile wide and certainly was no stranger to alcohol. But drinking alone in a motel room instead of at a party? That didn't sound like her at all.

"Then something's wrong." She grabbed the key from him and shoved it in the lock. "My sister does not party alone. Ever."

She shouldered the door open and gasped at the sight that greeted her. Her sister was indeed passed out on the bed, snoring, and the room not only reeked of alcohol it looked like it had exploded.

There were clothes, shoes, pictures, pretty much everything in the world her sister owned thrown all over the room. Not a single clear surface.

"What the hell? Rebel, wake up." Faith went straight for her sister and shook her shoulders. When she got nothing more than a mumble she turned back to Damien. "What happened to her? Why is she like this?" She pointed at the lump still lying in the bed not moving. She feared the worst. "My beautiful, vibrant sister does not drink herself to a stupor. Ever. She takes things in stride and keeps going. She has more will and strength than anyone I know. Not even when our parents died. While I was falling apart she took care of everything." She could feel the hysteria rising or maybe it was the lack of food or the wolf bite. But she was about to fall apart.

"We really should talk." He touched her shoulder and she flinched before whirling on him.

"We need to talk? About what? Does that have something to do with her? What the heck is going on?" There were so many unanswered questions she didn't know where to begin.

He grabbed her hand again and gently touched the bandage at her wrist. "It has to do with this mostly? And yes, your sister too. Once you understand what is going on then it will all make sense."

"You know why she is like this don't you? You need to spit it out because I literally cannot imagine what you could say that would make me understand this."

"Faaiitthh, is that you?" her sister slurred.

"Yes, Bel, it's me." She used her favorite old nickname from when they were little hoping it would get through all the alcohol soaked brain cells. "What's going on? Are you okay?"

"Youuu realllly shouldn't be heeerree. Not safffe."

Faith's body tensed, the hair on the back of her neck bristling. "What do you mean not safe? What are you talking about?" She brushed her sister's usually gorgeous, but now matted and sticky hair out of her eyes. "Talk to me, Bel."

"Werewolves on the island. Not safffe," Rebel repeated.

Faith shook her head. "You've definitely had too much to drink, sis. You're kind of right though. There are wolves on the island. I had a bit of a run in with one earlier." She held up her bandaged wrist. "Got the bite to prove it. Guess this means I'll need those lovely rabies shots."

Her sister's eyes widened. "Faith, you're not listening," she whispered. "Not just wolves. Men who change. I saw it with my own eyes."

"I'm sure you did." She patted Rebel on the shoulder and then rounded the bed to go to the bathroom. Her sister needed some water to drink and a cold rag. Under other circumstances she might suggest coffee to sober her up, but this was extreme. The best thing for her at this point would be sleep.

Out of sight of both her sister and the man who made her feel off kilter whenever she was around him, Faith grabbed her head and winced at the throbbing pain.

She wasn't feeling too hot either and didn't even get to blame it on an alcohol binge like her sister.

While she dug through the bathroom drawers searching for some aspirin to go along with the glass of water, Damien appeared in the doorway.

"We need to—" He didn't finish his sentence before he rushed forward to catch her when she swayed sideways. "You're not feeling well are you? Dammit, Faith. I need to know these things."

She shook her head. "I'll be fine. Just a little light headed is all. I skipped lunch and haven't had dinner yet."

"Uh-huh. Give them to me." He held out his hands.

She looked down at the empty glass and bottle of pain medication still gripped in her hands. "I'm fine. Really. I need to take care of Rebel."

"You need to sit down and let me handle this." His voice deepened, his tone clear he would take no more arguing.

"You're bossy," she said.

"It comes with the territory." He took the glass and filled it with water and then shook two aspirin from the bottle. "You first," he demanded.

When she hesitated, he sighed. "Don't worry. We'll take care of Rebel too. She may be a hot head pain in my ass, but I'm still kind of fond of her."

There was something about this situation that seemed off. He was being nice enough to her. Yet she got the feeling of being treated like a child, which resulted in her wanting to refuse his help and ignore the medication and water he offered.

With some effort she shook most of those feelings away and took the pills. The fact she wanted to get rid of this growing headache outweighed her desire to send Mr. bossy pants away.

When she handed the glass back to him he refilled it and disappeared through the door. She started to stand. It should be her helping her sister not some stranger. Yet the spots now wavering through her vision and the burning at her wrist had her rethinking her decision to move.

"The bite burns doesn't it?"

She jerked at the sound of his voice, surprised he'd crept up on her. "A little," she lied. It actually hurt quite a bit more than a little.

"It's going to get worse before it gets better."

"And you know this because you have experience with a wolf bite?" She didn't care that her skepticism showed. She was in a rinky dink hotel with a too hot to handle mysterious man who made her squirm and her drunk sister after having been attacked by a wolf in the middle of a foggy, deserted road on creep island.

No, that didn't sound crazy at all.

"You'd be surprised to know what all I have experience with, little one."

She could just imagine. The man ran a strip club for cripes sake.

"I would imagine that in your line of work there isn't much you haven't seen. But I don't see you getting a lot of wolves wandering through your doors looking for a cheap thrill."

His right brow lifted and the threat of a real smile lifted the edges of his mouth again. "You'd be surprised what will walk through my doors."

She rolled her eyes. Why did every word out of his mouth have to make him sound like sex on a stick? And why was she still so obsessed with sex around him?

Remembering something he said she almost missed, she looked up at him and asked, "Who is we?"

"What?"

"You said we'll take care of Rebel. Who is we?"

"My brother Dante is walking over. He's bringing food and coffee too."

"He didn't have to--"

Damien lifted his hand and brushed the hair that had fallen onto her forehead. "Yeah, he does. You and I can't stay here and someone needs to keep an eye on your sister until she recovers. So he's been designated."

She jumped from her perch on the edge of the tub and swayed forward. "I can take care of everything myself. We don't need babysitters."

Damien hauled her against him until she was steady on her feet. "I'm certain under normal circumstances you could do just about anything you set your mind to. You've definitely got a mind of your own. Unfortunately, there is nothing normal about that wolf bite and you and your sister will have to face a new reality after tonight."

His ominous warning raised the hair at the back of her neck and sent a shiver racing along her arms. This whole situation was beginning to feel a little stalkerish. "You know I get that you're Rebel's boss and all that, but you're not making any sense. What's the big frigging deal? My sister drank a little—well a lot— more tequila than she should have and I'm going to need a series of rabies shots in the morning. Tomorrow's going to suck, but we'll both live."

"You talk too much."

"I do no--" One minute she was delivering him a piece of her mind and the next his lips were covering hers and his warm tongue licking at the edges of her mouth. So many sensations exploded in her head she didn't know what to catalog first. Maybe it was the pillow soft touch of his lips against her own? Or maybe the scent of the outdoors mixed with his cologne. No, it was definitely the scratch of his neatly trimmed facial hair abrading her skin that consumed her. In fact, the sexy rub made her everything well south of her neck tingle.

She was still wrapping her brain around the new sensations when Damien drew back, abandoning the best kiss of her life as it barely got started.

"That's much better."

"Why did you do that?" she asked.

"Because I've been thinking about it for too long. And," he smiled, "It seemed like a good way to get you to shut up and listen."

She sighed. As much as her brain told her to argue and push him away, her body wouldn't allow it. "Fine. I'm listening."

"Not in here. Let's get you and Rebel settled and then I can explain."

"Fine. But this better be good. I don't want to be away from her for long."

The smile he'd hinted at finally broke free, transforming him into the most gorgeous male creature she'd ever encountered. How was that even possible?

"Don't worry, babe. It's always good."

FOUR

D amien heard the approach of his brother before he even got to the door. Wolf hearing came in handy like that. He left Faith to take care of her sister and went outside to talk to him. They had a lot to discuss and it was better done outside of earshot of either woman.

He glared at Dante as he approached. "What the hell is going on? I thought you were going to watch over her?"

"That woman is a pain in my ass. I tried to get her to listen to reason and she wanted nothing to do with anything I said. She kicked me out of her room and warned me not to come back. I was so pissed she's lucky I didn't do something drastic like tie her to the bed and leave her like that."

He grabbed the tray of coffee to go cups from Dante and moved a few feet farther from their window. He definitely didn't need to be overheard. "So you just tucked tail and ran instead of handling the situation? That isn't what I would have expected from you."

"Fuck no. I've been across the street at the diner this whole time. I stayed there and made sure she didn't go anywhere without me. You don't have to worry, I wasn't going to let her leave the island until she understood that our secrets have to stay here on the island. What's with the inquisition anyway? I thought we agreed to give her a few days to get used to the idea of our kind before we laid down any ultimatums."

"That's before her sister showed up and got herself bitten. The situation is half past out of control now."

Dante's eyes widened. "What? Are you serious? You bit her? I thought you wanted to stay away from her?"

Damien glared at him. "I'm not the asshole who did it. Jesus. Happened out on the bridge a couple of hours ago. She was attacked by someone else. The scents unfamiliar."

"You're thinking rogue?"

He nodded, knowing that replaying this event again would only agitate his wolf.

"Well, shit. Rebel's gonna freak if her sister turns furry on her before she's even had time to adjust. She may not act like it, but I think she's as protective of Faith as Faith is her."

He shook his head and took a quick swallow of coffee. "She's not going to turn. Without a mating bond it's highly unlikely."

"But not impossible. If she turns, we're going to have to hide. Cause our "employee" is going to come after us with a shotgun and she's not going to be satisfied until every one of us has an ass full of buck shot."

"We don't have to worry about that tonight. Rebel is so drunk she can barely stand let alone put two and two together no matter what she overhears. And then tomorrow you can remind her who's the boss and make her chill for a while."

Dante laughed. "You're crazy if you think she's going to roll over and play nice just because I tell her to. Why the hell do you think she's driving me nuts?"

"I think your mating season whipped and you'll do anything to get inside her pants."

"Screw you, Damien. You don't have room to talk. You're out here talking to me instead of inside taking care of the woman you want but won't touch. That's fucked dude."

He sipped at his coffee and glared at his brother who glared right back. Unfortunately, they had better things to do than stand out here and measure dicks and Dante wasn't exactly wrong. He did want Faith.

He also wanted to kill the rogue wolf who dared to sink teeth in her. Another man's scent on her skin was driving him mad. As was the idea she'd been marked by a stranger instead of him.

Dante touched his shoulder, his voice lowering. "It doesn't have to end here you know. She's been bitten without a bond. Even if she turns, she'll still choose her own mate."

He nodded, unwilling to say anything more. In the midst of mating season he wasn't sure he could trust himself with Faith's well being.

Not when all he could think about was how she smelled both sweet and exciting. Or how just being next to her set his already pounding heart to racing. She even made him want to spend the night just kissing her. She licked her full red lips earlier and since then he'd been plagued by images of that luscious mouth wrapped around his cock. He couldn't get it out of his head.

"If that wolf is anywhere nearby, he's going to want to find her. He'll follow her scent, which is going to lead him right here. You should know I'm going to have a problem with that."

Dante's words not only shook him from his lascivious thoughts, they down right pissed him off. "Let him come. I'd be happy to divest him of his beating heart," he growled.

His brother held up his hands. "Don't shoot the damned messenger. I'm not telling you anything you don't know is true. I just want to make sure you're listening. Someone else marking the woman you want is going to mess with your head. You need to fight it."

He closed his eyes and took a deep breath. It wasn't his intention to take it out on Dante, and he was right. "A rogue wolf running loose on our island is a serious problem. We need to find him before he finds her."

"You tell her yet?"

"No." He wasn't looking forward to doing it either.

Dante whistled. "I sure hope she takes the news better than her sister did. Otherwise we'll both be watching them from a distance."

"Like hell. Not only is she nothing like Rebel, she's not getting ten feet from me whether she likes it or not."

His brother snickered. "Good luck with that dude. Faith seems like the silent, quiet type, but I have a feeling when riled that won't be the case. Those two women are cut from the same cloth whether we like it or not."

"The simple solution is to find our intruder. We need to start making some calls and get security hopping around here. Have you heard from Creed or Sawyer?"

"Our security has seemingly gone off the radar since mating season began. Not that I blame them. I'll call them both though, but don't be surprised when they rip us a new one."

"I can handle their attitudes. Plus, we all know how important this is. They'll get on board. What about the others?"

He shrugged again. "You know how it is. We give everyone us much leeway as we can during this time. If they haven't found a connection, they'll be here."

That would have to be good enough. "We should be able to handle it. Just make sure everyone knows to stay on alert just in case." How much trouble could one rogue wolf be? As soon as the thought popped into his head he knew he was going to regret thinking that.

"Yeah," Dante agreed. "I don't think the wolf is your biggest problem right now." They both glanced in the direction of where he'd left Faith alone with her sister.

He was probably right, but standing outside a motel room debating the situation wasn't going to help either.

He headed back to the room, "Then let's deal with this shit."

CHAPTER

FIVE

Faith sighed when she heard the door opening again. Her wish that Damien would leave and let her deal with Rebel on her own had been too much to hope for. Although the fact he walked in carrying a tray of coffee cups helped--a little.

"What are you--?" Her question died on her lips when Damien moved in the room and his brother Dante followed him. Just as tall and broad as Damien, it was no wonder Rebel liked her job. And now she understood why he bothered her so much. It was kind of like how Damien unnerved her. They both oozed testosterone and some kind of male magnetism that was hard to describe. Whatever it was, she imagined neither of these men lacked in female companionship.

"Faith this is Dante. Dante, Faith."

"Hey." He smiled and held up two bags in his hands. "Hungry?"

She shrugged and eyeballed the coffee cups instead. "Is one of those for me?"

"Absolutely, take your pick. There's sugar and creamer in the bag if you need it." Dante stepped forward and offered her the tray. "Damien tells me you've had a rough night."

"Understatement of the year." She sipped gently at the cup, testing the heat level before gulping some of it down.

"Our island's not usually a hotbed of trouble on a Monday night," Dante winked at her. "It seems the rising moon is wreaking all kinds of havoc."

Her eyebrows raised. "If you say so. But I've always found the island to be a bit of an enigma. You may not be that far from the city, but you might as well be a thousand miles away. It's like visiting another culture."

"That's a whole lot of opinion formed from one wolf bite." Damien interjected, his eyebrows drawn together with a look that had annoyance written all over it.

"Speaking of which... I think that's our cue to part ways. I'm going to stay here and keep an eye on Rebel here so you can go with Damien."

She looked between her sleeping sister and this man she barely knew. "Why in the world would I go anywhere but here? I came to your lovely little rock to find out what's going on with my sister and that's what I intend to do."

Damien stepped forward and placed his hands on her shoulders. That firm, strong touch caught her off guard again. She looked up and her gaze collided with his. The usually vivid green hue of his eyes had darkened, making it impossible to read anything. But his intensity heightened and her skin tingled at their connection.

"You're not safe here."

Faith gulped for air. His body this close to hers short circuited her ability to think and form complete sentences without a lot of effort. "Why am I not safe? I don't understand."

"I'd rather explain that when I'm certain you are secure. We need to leave."

This was crazy. She wasn't going to jump just because he was ridiculously good looking.

Liar. She'd probably do just about anything if he asked, including lick his entire body.

Her mind might reject her thought shenanigans, but her body certainly didn't. Her skin sizzled from head to toe at the thought of something--anything happening between them.

Talk about inappropriate.

"I'm not going anywhere with you," she pointed at Damien, "or him," she hooked her thumb at his equally ridiculously good looking brother, "unless someone gives me a damn good reason. Like an epically good reason."

The two men exchanged knowing glances and her stomach dropped. She had a feeling she wasn't going to like what they were about to say.

"Do it, Damien. You need to quit wasting time. If the rogue is coming for her, it won't take him long to pick up her trail here."

"Who's coming for me?" she asked. "And what on earth for? I'm nobody."

Damien turned back to her and she would swear he managed to turn the intensity up by several notches. "You have never been a nobody, but tonight you became prey. The wolf that bit you wasn't an ordinary wolf. He's a shapeshifter. Part human, part wolf and all predator. I can smell it on you."

Faith took several steps back. Obviously good looking came with a drawback. Crazy. And lots of it.

Greeeaaattt.

"I know it sounds ridiculous and unbelievable, but trust me. What I'm saying is true."

Dante's head nodded, "He's right. We need to get you somewhere more secure."

"No, no. This is crazy." Why did they keep looking at her like that? As if she was a child who couldn't comprehend reality. She knew reality just fine and it wasn't some fairytale gone nuts. Wolves don't turn into humans.

"I think Rebel should get off this island immediately and go home with me. "

"No." Both men said in unison. "You wouldn't last five minutes if you tried to leave Devils Point alone." Damien took a few steps closer. "I'm sorry it had to be like this, but we'll do whatever it takes to keep you safe. Even if that means we have to save you from yourself."

Fear sliced through her at the chill of his words and the demanding tone of his voice. Now she understood why he made her feel so unsettled. It wasn't just an air of strong masculinity like she'd thought. It was danger.

She wrapped her arms around her waist and tried to think. Her sister was passed out on the bed and somehow she needed to get them both past two large and determined men that stood between her and the door. In hindsight she now wished she'd taken that self defense class her freshman year. Campus security had strongly urged new students take the course and she'd scoffed at them. Her idea of safety was a locked door behind the walls of a secure apartment complex and that had served her well for four long years.

Suddenly the ache in her wrist began to burn. Not a little "ouch that stings", but an honest to God, "holy fuck that hurts." She grabbed the bandage and pressed down on it, while stumbling backward as her body swayed to the side. Why did her skin feel like it was on fire?

"What's wrong?" Damien rushed forward and caught her around the waist before she crashed to the floor.

"Skin--skin's on fire," she gasped.

Damien swept her into his arms and carried her into the bathroom. He turned the cold faucet on, ripped her bandage off and shoved her arm under the running water. At first she cried out and tried to pull free, but he held her steady and after several long seconds some of the burning receded.

"It's already infected isn't it?" Faith wiped the tears from her cheeks and looked down at her wrist. The wound was bright red, but she couldn't tell anything else.

"Your body is trying to expel the wolf's enzymes. The animal DNA strand is very strong and often overpowers a human."

"Am I going to get sick?" She was still ignoring the fact they expected her to believe she'd been bitten by some kind of human/animal shifter. But an animal bite of any kind carried risks.

"Probably. This kind of bite isn't as well documented as one during mating. It has to be watched."

"I don't want to--" Pain cramped her stomach and she tried to turn away as the meager contents of her stomach came hurling out in a horrific projectile way. Tears sprang to her eyes and sweat popped out all over her as her body heaved, trying to get rid of everything inside her. Or at least that's how it felt.

"Shit."

Damien moved behind her and she wanted to disappear. He grabbed a washcloth from the cabinet, wet it under the faucet and to her horror began washing her. She wanted to object, fight this somehow. Anything to end her humiliation and she couldn't. She was too weak.

He propped her against his chest and careful not to touch her wound, he cleaned her face, chest and arms. "I'm taking you home."

She tried to object but the sound came out as barely a whimper.

"Don't waste your energy. I know. You won't leave your sister. She's coming too. Dante will bring her."

Faith nodded. What else could she do? This brilliant trip had officially kicked her ass.

And for some strange reason (despite his crazy) she strangely trusted Damien to keep her safe. Maybe because he'd been her sister's boss for months and other than the fact he peddled flesh for a living, he didn't seem so bad.

Or maybe it was that Rebel trusted them. She didn't just work on this island. She lived here and refused to leave no matter how much Faith tried to convince her stubborn sister that this was no life for her. There had to be something to that. Had to be. Or she'd failed their parents big time...

CHAPTER
SIX

Damien sensed the moment Faith woke up. She hadn't moved a muscle but her breathing had changed and since she was currently in his bed with his body curled around hers, he saw, heard and felt everything. For example, her heart beat had quickened and now her muscles were taught.

"Easy, Faith. It's just me," he whispered into her ear, not bothering to mask the desire coursing through him when he spoke. "How do you feel?"

"I don't know. It's kind of hard to tell with you laying on top of me."

He chuckled and tightened his hold. He wasn't ready to lose her quite yet. "I was keeping you warm. Your fever broke hours ago and I didn't want you to get cold.

She started to stir, which resulted in her panty covered bottom rubbing across his very hard groin. She froze. He bit his lips to keep from laughing.

"It's first thing in the morning, what did you expect to feel?"

Her heart was beating faster and her breathing shallow. He inhaled deep, taking in the scents throughout the room. At least this time she didn't smell like fear. That agitated his wolf and the last thing he needed to do right now was agitate anything.

He did however, scent the faintest touch of arousal blossoming across her skin. Unable to resist her, he buried his face between her shoulder blades and lapped at the silken flesh that taunted him most of the night.

"What are you doing?" She asked, although he noted she did not try to move away like he expected.

"You smell good. I wanted a taste."

The scent of her arousal got stronger and he smiled.

"How long have I been here?"

"Just since last night. Your fever spiked and broke within the span of six hours. I think the worst is over."

She wiggled her body through his arms and this time he let her go. As far as he was concerned they had time to get where they needed to be. Provided of course, his pack located the rogue and put him down before he caused any more trouble.

He'd been attracted to this woman since the first time they'd met, a fact that used to annoy him. Her humanity didn't bother him. Her need for a simple, safe life did. He thrived on the unknown and relished a hunt that involved danger.

But since she'd been bitten, it seemed fate had stepped in and made him an offer he couldn't refuse. If he didn't claim her someone else in the pack would. And that didn't settle well with him at all. Fuck that.

She looked down at her wrist and then held it up. "What about this? Is it okay?"

"Yes and no."

She placed her unmarked hand on her hip and cocked her eyebrows at him. A saucy smirk from a sweet woman. That made for a heady mix. And unlike her sister, she didn't seem to have that wild, screw the establishment and I hate the world, streak. Thank goodness. He liked Rebel just fine and she was one hell of a popular stripper in their club, but she was a handful in all the wrong ways.

"Where's Rebel?"

"Not here. She went out hunting with the rest of the pack."

"Hunting? Hunting for what?" Her voice rose several octaves, hurting his ears.

He covered his head with a pillow to muffle the sound. "Dante and the rest of the pack are out looking for the wolf that bit you."

"What?" She shrieked.

He winced. "Jesus, Faith. Shit. Take pity and never do that again."

She continued at the same high pitched volume. "You mean scream at you because you let my sister go out there," she pointed through the window, "and hunt for a wild animal that could kill her. Seriously?!"

He reluctantly pulled the pillow from around his ears and sat up. "She's with the pack. They're not going to let anything happen to her. Besides, do you know your sister? The minute the pack showed up here she was going and nothing short of tying her down *and* locking her up was going to keep her off the hunt."

"Why do you keep saying pack? Who is the pack? Your friends? Your work people? What does that mean?"

Thankfully she didn't scream those questions at him.

"My pack is everyone. My friends, my family, everyone who lives in Devils Point who is like me." He said all the words. He wasn't even sure if she remembered their discussion from the night before but they had to get it out in the open sooner rather than later so she could deal with it in case she still turned.

"Like you. What does that mean?"

"Do you remember what I said last night about your wolf bite. How he wasn't an ordinary wolf." He braced for her reaction, expecting more screaming.

Faith rolled her eyes. "Damien, don't do this. I was feeling pretty good about being out here with you. You taking care of me when I got sick was one of the sweetest things anyone has ever done for me. Don't ruin it with nonsense. Please."

The sadness and exasperation in her voice tore at his heart. She didn't believe him. That part didn't surprise him. It wasn't an easy revelation to swallow. But the disappointment that she felt because she thought he was letting her down cut deep.

He knew why he protected Rebel so much despite her crazy antics. It was the same reason he felt a connection to Faith. They lost their pack a long time ago and neither one of them realized that together they could still be whole. As long as they had each other they would be fine. At least as soon as they got it through their thick skulls.

She was still standing there staring down at the ground. The scent of sadness cloaked her, and somehow she was using it like a protective blanket. To keep him out.

The only way she'd ever believe would be to see. And to see would mean she'd have to deal. This is what Dante meant with her sister.

"Do you trust me that I will never hurt you?"

Her head jerked up. "That's a really weird question right now. I barely know you."

"I think you know me better than you think. Rebel knows me. No one in my family would ever allow you or her to be hurt. I need you to believe that."

Tears shimmered in her eyes looking at him. "I think I do. I can't really explain why but I do."

He yearned to pull her close. Envelop her in his embrace and press her luscious curvy body into his hard frame. But they were finally getting somewhere so he needed to stop thinking about peeling her t-shirt off and laying her back down in his bed so he could devour her--slowly.

He cleared his throat. "Look at me, Faith."

"I am," she responded.

He got up and took a few steps in her direction until he could reach out and cup her chin. "Look at me."

Thankfully, she did what he asked and lifted her head so she could focus on his eyes. Without further preamble he pulled on the strength of the inner wolf just enough to make his eyes change. Nothing too extreme. While his vision sharpened, she only sees the subtle color changes from green to gold.

Her breath hitched. "Your--your eyes. They're beautiful."

She sounded surprised but not scared and so far there was no scent of fear. Instead the way she studied him made him want to lean forward and capture her lips. Maybe pull her soft, gently rounded belly against his aching cock.

All thoughts he needed to stop having before this discussion derailed. They had to get through this before he could tell her that part.

"They're the eyes of my wolf. Like the one who bit you, I too can change. Part human, part wolf. My choice."

She stood transfixed, staring into his eyes. Both seeing and not seeing at the same time.

"It's not possible," she said. "That's made up fantasy."

"No baby, it's not. If you need me to I can show you. But I really don't want to scare you. You've been through enough in one day."

And it was mating season. His wolf wanted her as bad as the rest of him. And this time of year the wolf had a way of getting exactly what he wanted.

SEVEN

Faith didn't know what to do. She harbored no secret beliefs in otherworldly beings or supernatural anything, but here she stood staring at the compelling yellow glow of his eyes while he told her he was what... a werewolf?

"You've stumbled into wolf country during mating season I'm afraid. The wolf that bit you is not part of my pack though. But rogue or not, we're all going through the same thing. The desire to mate and reproduce is almost impossible to control."

"This is about sex then."

He closed his eyes and shook his head, a low growl sounding from deep within his chest. "Most of us do spend the season searching and having sex. The odds of finding the right person to mate with are slim, so we relieve some of the tension other ways.

But the actual mating is far more than sex. It's a connection, a bond between mates that intertwines two people together for the rest of their lives. Like marriage but more. Especially when it comes to true mates. That's such a rare connection half of us don't believe in it unless we experience it."

Her brain hurt. All of this information was sending her into overload. "I need to sit down." She stumbled to the bed and sat down hard, finding it difficult to do or say anything smoothly.

She caught sight of her bandaged wrist and lifted it up. "Am I going to become a werewolf because of this? Is that what all of this is about?"

"It's a definite possibility, You got pretty ill and your fever spiked so you're definitely affected. I'm hoping since you woke up feeling better that it won't go south from here. But turning a human can be complicated. In some cases it only takes a bite and in others it takes a bond to form between shifter and human first."

"Sex," she whispered.

"Sometimes. If a connection is made. It's kind of hard to explain."

"I think I'm getting it. I just don't know what to make of it. Are you saying the wolf who bit me was planning to mate me?"

The dark look that crossed Damien's face startled her. That sense of danger she felt before returned. It made her wonder how ruthless he could be.

"It won't matter after I rip his throat out for hurting you. And he's damn lucky you didn't die last night or I would do worse than put him out of his misery."

Her mouth fell open. The ease at which he talked about violence made her uneasy. "I could have died from just a bite?"

"That's the point of the bond. It makes you more compatible. Without it, anything can happen."

She took a few steps away from him. "I think I need to go home now and take some time to think about all this. And I don't feel very safe on this island at the moment." She turned away and started planning her escape. First she had to find her clothes and shoes. "I need to take Rebel with me."

"I doubt she'll go. She's made a home here. She's connected."

"I hardly consider a long term room in a shabby motel a home. She's been going wild for years now and it's time for her--" she whirled around and faced Damien.

"Wait? Are you telling me that she knows about this--uh--werewolf/shapeshifter thing?" It really felt weird to say it out loud.

He nodded, a slight move that seemed reluctant. "She accidentally saw Dante change behind the club a few nights ago."

"So that's why she wasn't at work." It was all starting to make so much more sense.

"And probably why she was at the bottom of a bottle yesterday," he said. "Every human who learns our secret has to deal with it in their own way."

Jeez. She'd walked--or driven--into one hell of a mess. "All the more reason for me to go home and take my sister with me. She's out of control. I couldn't stand the thought of her stripping in your club in the first place. That she's surrounded by danger makes it even worse. Why would a werewolf own a place like that anyway? Wouldn't you prefer a job in nature or something? Don't you need to be outside?"

"Great. Now we get to start with the cliches." he laughed. "Faith, you're adorable, but you've got a long way to go before you really understand what we are. We're just as much human as we are wolf, maybe even a little more. So we have hopes and dreams that extend beyond running through the woods all day and hunting prey. Although don't get me wrong, we really love those things too. But my point is, we live semi normal lives and we strive to fit in as much as possible. In order to do that we have to make money to buy land, homes, clothing and more just like everyone else. We even go to school."

"That's not what I meant. I just thought with a special power everything might be different somehow." she hesitated. "So your big dream was to own a strip club and peddle naked women to desperate men?"

His eyes shuttered closed for a moment as he took a deep breath. "Club Diablo serves many purposes and the men and women we employ are there because they want to be, not because they were coerced. I'm a little disappointed you feel the need to judge us like that."

Dammit. He was right of course. She had no right to judge anyone. Her life experiences didn't exactly include the best judgement calls. Her freshman year of college had gone pretty wrong. Starting with losing her virginity to a douche bag and then following it up with a string of jerks who she thought would keep her safe while getting into her pants. It had taken getting accidentally drugged at a frat party to wake her up to reality.

"I'm sorry," she said. "I'm biased. It's not easy to accept my twin actually wants this life. I can't wrap my head around her taking her clothes off every night for any dude with cash in his hand. We're supposed to be connected and I don't feel that at all anymore. Not since..." She let the sentence die. She didn't want to say it out loud.

"Everyone deals with grief in their own way. Besides, it pays really well. A lot of women like that. They usually save it up quick and then move on."

"Rebel doesn't need money. Our parents left us with a life insurance policy that she refuses to touch."

"Then talk to her about it. Your acceptance of her choices would probably straighten some things out. She's dealing with the same hardships you are in her own way."

Faith scrubbed her hands over her face and then looked up at him again. "So what other purpose does Club Diablo serve? You said there were more."

"Well," he hesitated. "Humans have hang ups about sex that wolves don't. We own most of the island except some acreage owned by the state where the park is. That draws tourists which is okay as long as they don't stay too long. So an island known for its dirty sex club is a deterrent for humans to settle here. Some still come and go, but for the most part our island consists of pack. And thanks to Diego's bright idea a few years back to turn our place into a male strip show on special occasions, we use it during mating season to meet more women in the hopes of finding a mate."

She wrinkled up her nose at that idea. "Cause that's not sketchy at all."

"Its a hell of a lot safer for us to be on home ground during the season. The last thing we need is a horny, needy were roaming random city streets looking for women out of his control without his pack to back him up. That's how rogues happen and pretty girls get bitten on the side of the road."

"Touche."

He stepped forward and brushed her cheek with his fingers. "You'll learn. It's safer when we stick to our pack. Similar to the way you need your twin."

A shiver worked down her spine as the sensation of his touch ghosted across her skin. He didn't play fair at all.

"I still think I should go home. The smart thing to do would be to consider everything you've told me, weigh my options."

"Your option is to stay here. Become part of the Devils Point wolves. To leave the safety of the pack makes you fair game to others. You've been marked. And even if you don't fully change, you won't be fully human either. You'll be subject to the mating season every year too and the others out there like us will find you. Either way you'll be forced to choose a mate. It's in the DNA."

"I don't like being told what to do, Damien. I learned that lesson the hard way."

"Oh make no mistake, the choice is yours. Fate deals you a hand and you can either embrace the gift you're given or fight your way down a different path. And most wolves will honor that."

"Most? That doesn't sound like a choice at all."

"It's life. Werewolf or human, we are not created equal and there are assholes in every bunch. Wolves just have that extra animal instinct that drives them during the season."

"I don't know what to do here," she admitted.

"I could offer you some incentive to stay." He smiled down at her, reminding her once again how ridiculously good looking he was when he did that.

"I'm listening." She rubbed her hands on her plump thighs suddenly feeling a bit self conscious. She couldn't wait to hear what he said next.

EIGHT

"I've wanted you since the first time I saw you. It didn't matter that you didn't seem my type or that I didn't think I'd ever be ready to find a mate. Or that you were too young. You lived inside me as a living, breathing ache. The only thing that saved either of us was the fact you lived far enough away I rarely saw you. It allowed me to keep on going and doing my own thing. Except during mating season."

Faith didn't know what to say. She ached right now too. All she could think about was his hands touching her everywhere. Or maybe his lips working their way across all of her most sensitive zones. The fact he stood there in nothing but a pair of black pants unfastened at the waist made it impossible not to think about more.

"I do have a nice apartment in a secure building. I feel safe there," she blurted.

He seemingly ignored her when he spoke again, "Mating season drives an ordinary wolf crazy. But one that knows he has a mate out there goes a little mad." His fingers trailed down the side of her neck, past her shoulders and down the side of her torso, just grazing the outside of her breast.

"And you think I'm your mate?" She whispered.

"The wolf says so and the more I get to know you I'm inclined to agree." He leaned forward and pressed his lips to hers in a gentle kiss. They both moaned simultaneously.

Everything about him turned her on, even the dangerous wolf she didn't fully comprehend.

"If you don't want this, you have to stop me. Being here right now hurts me." Before she formed the question he continued, "Mating season is a bitch. It makes me want to fuck or die. It's hard to control."

"That's not very sexy."

"Sorry, babe. The wolf says you're the one, I'm feeling it too and the mark on your wrist makes the need to claim you even more intense."

Faith couldn't really argue his point. She'd felt the pull all along, she just wouldn't admit it. Whether he wanted to call it instinct or she called it lust didn't really matter. Either way she wanted to give into it.

"Take off your pants," she said.

A look crossed his face and then disappeared just as fast. As did his pants. Quickly followed by his underwear.

Tall, muscular and aroused. Holy hell.

"Your turn."

She hesitated for a second, remembering her flaws. A little belly and a few extra pounds didn't seem so bad until you were standing in front of a perfect specimen. She took a deep breath and lifted the shirt over her head and tossed it to the ground. He seemed to want her flaws and all and who was she to pass up a moment like this for any lame reason.

"What's so funny?"

"Nothing, why?"

"You're grinning." He pulled her closer again and peppered kisses along her shoulders and neck, his fingers brushing the sides of her breasts. "Beautiful," he whispered, sliding his thumbs across her already tightening nipples.

When Damien bent down and tugged one of them with his teeth, the need inside her coalesced, making her pliant and wet.

"You probably say that to all the women you're trying to get in bed."

He laughed. "It's no secret I've loved women. Shifters are sexual creatures. But you, Faith, are extraordinary. You're the woman made for me and you were made perfectly."

Oh wow. "That was really good, Damien." She reached down and wrapped her hand around his cock. And what a hefty beauty it was. "You are about to get very lucky."

Damien groaned. "Hell yes." His big hands reached down and cupped her butt and pulled them together as much as he could while her thumb rubbed over his tip.

Faith shivered under the onslaught. Coming to this island was starting to not look so bad after all.

"Are you going to bite me tonight?"

Damien pulled back, meeting her gaze. "Do you want me to?"

"You said you've wanted me since the day we first met. Is that true?"

He nodded. "More so than you can imagine."

"I had dreams about you. Some were sexual, but some weren't. But one night--" she paused, feeling insecure.

"One night you bit my neck and told me I belonged to you. It felt so real I tried to call Rebel the next morning to ask about you. That was the first night she didn't respond to my calls. Three nights later I had to come. For her. And for you."

"That was the first night of mating season. Things weren't going so well here. The need for you was so painful I tried to get in my car and drive to Seattle. It took Dante shifting into his wolf to subdue me. That's when Rebel came out the back door of the club and saw us."

Faith's mind reeled from this new information. They were connected long before she got bitten by some half assed wolf. This was real. And she couldn't wait another minute to have him.

She reached up and pushed his chest as hard as she could. Fortunately, he was caught off balance or he went with it, but either way he tumbled back on the bed and she crawled on top to straddle him. He was perfectly hard and she was seriously ready. She grasped his shaft and lifted over him.

Damien grabbed her hips. "I do like a wild woman who isn't afraid to take what she needs," he growled.

She leaned forward and kissed his lips. "Good. Because tonight is the night you're going to bite me. I'm not going to pretend I need time to be sure or second guess my choice until I'm riddled with doubt. *I know.* I claim you as my mate." She shifted her hips until his tip nestled at her opening. His grip on her hips tightened, keeping them both on the brink.

Their eyes locked and he slowly pulled her down on him.

Holy fucking hell. She flung her head back and wailed at the pleasure. Damien was huge, but her body was ready as it stretched to accommodate him. Everything inside her went haywire. She kept her eyes open and watched his face. The wolf still glowed in his eyes, but the rest of him was all man. Incredible, hard, amazing man who wasted no time moving his hands to her breasts to pull at her nipples. The fiery heat of sudden pain mixed with the all consuming pleasure between her legs to tip her over the edge.

His hands returned to her waist with a fierce, demanding grip as his hips drove up into her again and again. She might have been on top but he controlled everything.

"Harder, Faith." he commanded as he shoved deep inside her. Eager to give him what he needed, she quickened her pace, throwing her head back again and riding him with everything she had. Moments later he was still fucking her but he also pulled her down to kiss him. With lips locked and sweat slickened bodies pressed together, he rolled her on the bed until she was underneath him.

His thrusts continued and she grabbed onto his back for leverage to meet them. Her nails dug into his skin and he groaned. Every move he made sent fresh pleasure pulses shooting through her as he made love to her. Out of this world mad, wild love.

When her orgasm hit, it caught her by surprise. Everything around her disappeared except Damien. Her head spun out of control.

"Damien."

"Fuck yes, baby. Squeeze my dick. Take what's yours."

With her body convulsing, Damien leaned down and kissed her neck in several places before replacing his lips with the points of his teeth. "I claim you too," he said on a hoarse whisper before sinking his fangs into her skin.

With his mouth locked onto her neck, he thrust deep and groaned.

Heat filled her as her new mate found his release, while still pounding into her. When Damien finally collapsed on her, his mouth popped free from her neck and they both panted, unable to catch their breath.

Damien rolled over on the bed and Faith grinned as he gathered her in his arms. It had been so long since she felt this happy she wasn't sure she recognized it. Other than it felt really really good.

She'd dreamed of one day finding a husband and settling down, but this--it was so much more. "That was incredible."

"Yep. Blew my mind," he said. "When do you want to do it again?"

Faith leaned into his side and laughed. "Shifters are insatiable aren't they?"

Damien lifted his head and sifted his fingers through her hair. "Pretty much. Hope thats not a problem."

"Hardly. Although I might need a minute to catch my breath."

He hugged her closer and kissed her cheek. "We've got all the time in the world."

Faith froze, her breath catching in her throat. Tears suddenly stung her eyes.

"Baby, what's wrong?"

She shook her head. "My father used to say that to my mother. That they had all the time in the world." Her breath hitched. "I'm sorry it's silly."

"No, Faith. It's not. I'm so sorry for you loss. For both you and your sister. Losing a parent is one of the worst things that can happen. Losing them both at the same time. I don't even know…" His voice trailed off and she couldn't help but think he was getting lost in his own thoughts. So she pulled him back.

"I love and miss my parents, but even harder is the feeling I've lost my twin. We were so close before. I've become different without her and I don't mean in a better way. I get scared a lot. And I struggle with feeling safe."

"I've noticed you mentioned that. You'll feel safe here once you get used to us all. The pack protects their own. You're pack now." He was tracing patterns on her lower back and it felt really good. His touch calmed her, made her start to feel drowsy.

She nestled deeper into his arms, where she could soak up more of his warmth. She did feel safer here. "I hope you're right. But I still miss her. I need her to be okay."

Damien used his finger to lift her chin until her lips met his. "Of course you do, baby. You wouldn't be you if you didn't. Now kiss me so we can go to sleep because I have a feeling things are going to get better soon."

NINE

Damien rolled over when the faint sound of his cell phone woke him. He fished it out of his pants and checked the caller ID, pressing the answer button as soon as he saw Diego's name.

"You've got incoming," his brother blurted before he uttered a word.

"Who?"

"Rebel, and she's on the warpath. Dante collared your rogue, but not before he told the whole pack that your woman was marked. She attacked him herself and it took two of us to drag her off of him. She still got off a shot and the wolf's got a nice sized hole in his leg."

"Fuck. I knew that woman would be trouble."

"Always is. Doesn't change facts though. We'd better get used to her."

Damien sighed. Things were still fragile between him and Faith. He'd laid everything on the line with her earlier and after a bit of an inquisition and a hell of a wild time in bed, she accepted him. The last thing she needed right now was to have to choose sides. Rebel was family and he knew as well as anyone, you protected your family at all costs.

"Thanks for letting me know." He ended the call and stood, grabbing his pants from the floor.

"What's going on?" Faith asked, her voice behind him soft from sleep. Made him want to crawl back in bed and bite her again. While he was fucking her of course.

"Nothing serious. You stay here and rest. You'll need it for when I come back."

"Promise?" she asked.

"Definitely, my little wild thing. I'll be right back."

He headed to the front door but before he could open it, it came crashing open, slamming against the wall. It would have bounced back closed except Rebel slammed her booted foot against the wood and held it open.

Red hair, tangled and wild, swirled around her head as she locked her anger filled gaze on his. "Hey asshole."

His favorite wicked witch had arrived.

"You lied to me. Told me Faith would be fine and she'd be safe with you. Where is she? In your fucking bed?" She lowered the shotgun propped against her shoulder and pointed it at his heart.

"Dammit, Rebel. Your sister is fine. She's safer here than anywhere else in the world. You should know that." He took a deep breath and reached for some calm. He could move a hell of a lot quicker than the woman in front of him, but he couldn't take the chance she'd be hurt.

She shook her head. "I know you lied. Again. I'm not sure anymore that any of you can be trusted."

"What's going on out here?" Faith ran into the room with a sheet wrapped around her lush frame.

"Aaaahhhh!" Rebel yelled, her finger moving to the trigger of the gun. "Liar," she screamed. "She had a life. A safe and happy one. And you stole her! This is not where she is supposed to be."

Faith stepped between him and the gun and he growled. "Get out of the way, Faith."

"Shut up!" They both yelled at him.

"Rebel Jayne Harris, what the hell is wrong with you? Put that gun down and start explaining yourself." Faith had her hands on her hips giving her sister what for and all he could think about was that she belonged to him now.

Mine. The wolf growled.

"You don't belong here. You have a life in Seattle. You're going to be a scientist. You can't be one of them now. You can't go off the rails, that's my job."

"Good lord. No pressure. Since when did I end up on a pedestal with the perfect life? Are you crazy? My life has not been perfect. I lost the same things you did and I had to struggle through that on my own. Alone. Now I've chosen a different path and suddenly you're going to freak out and claim to know what's best for me?"

Rebel lifted her chin and sniffed. "You've been trying to manage me for years. I think I'm due."

Faith sighed and walked up to her sister. "You don't need this here." She grabbed the gun from Rebel and handed it back to him. It was then he realized he'd been holding his breath watching these two women argue.

"Why don't we go in the kitchen and I'll fix us all something to drink." He certainly needed it.

His mate turned and threw him a grateful smile. "Make it alcoholic and you've got a deal."

"Done," he said. Leading the women through the living room of his cabin he thought about how boring this place was. He'd gone to a lot of trouble building the place with all reclaimed wood and the best construction materials money could buy and then never taken the time to properly furnish or decorate the place, instead filling it with castoffs from other pack members and the requisite bachelor leather furniture and big screen television.

Since he spent most of his time at Club Diablo it never bothered him until now. Time to implement some changes. He settled the women at the large kitchen island and went to work on fixing their drinks. He had the ingredients for the usual margaritas and mojitos that his patrons and guests ordered, but this situation called for something different. So he pulled out three tumblers, filled a bucket with ice and a bottle of Disaronno.

"Rebel, you gotta find a way to deal with this. It's too late for me to turn back now. That boat sailed the minute that rogue wolf bit me."

"How do you know this asshole right here didn't trick you all along and he was the mysterious rogue out on the bridge who took the chunk out of you? He's pretty convincing, but he's also willing to do just about anything to get what he wants."

"Hey!" he objected.

"That's absurd. He barely knew me. Besides, no one but you could have known I was coming to the island that night. I told no one except your voicemail."

"Make him prove it. He can shift into a wolf and you should be able to tell whether he was the wolf that attacked you or not."

"I will no--"

"I'll do it." Anything to get Rebel down from her latest rampage. "But," he turned to Rebel, "when I prove it wasn't me, you have to get chilled. You've been hysterical for days and it's getting old. We're wolves not mutant zombies here to eat your fucking brains."

Rebel huffed. "I'll do what I can, but I'm not ruling out some freak of nature alien bullshit."

Damien shook his head and walked over to his mate's sister draping his arm across her shoulder. "That's Sir alien to you. You're still my employee."

"Hopefully not for long," Faith mumbled while taking a sip of her drink.

He moved into the middle of the living room and began unbuttoning his shirt. He then unfastened his jeans and slid them down his legs. When he reached for his underwear, Faith shrieked.

"Do you have to take it all off?"

Rebel snickered. "He sure does."

"If I'm wearing clothes when I shift they pretty much get shredded and ruined. I'll turn around how about that?"

His mate nodded, but the stricken look on her face remained. She really had no idea how not a big deal this was. There wasn't a person in the pack who hadn't already seen everything. They often shifted and ran together and naked in their human form was pretty standard by the end of the night.

"Don't worry, sis. It's not anything I haven't already seen."

"Not helping," Faith seethed through clenched teeth.

Ready to get this over with, he pulled on the strength of his wolf until he felt fur moving under his skin and then pushing through. It wasn't going to be this easy for Faith the first time she shifted. He remembered that moment as painful and not fun at all. But with him there to ease her transition he was confident it wouldn't be that bad.

"What the hell is going on here?"

Damien sighed at the sound of Dante's voice behind him. Was there no sacred space among pack that he couldn't take his clothes off without someone new showing up unannounced?

"Damien here is going to shift into his wolf form and prove to Faith that he is not the rogue wolf who bit her. At least not the first time."

Dante's eyes widened. "You mated her? Hell to the fucking yeah, it's about goddamn time." Dante grabbed him by the shoulders and pulled him into a hug.

"Uhm could we do this after I get my clothes back on?" He pulled free from his brother and scooped his pants from the floor and yanked them back up his legs.

"This is ridiculous. Rebel doesn't need proof you're not the one who bit her sister, she confronted the asshole responsible and even shot him.

Faith jumped from her stool. "You did what?"

"What's the big deal. He'll heal. Isn't that what you magical werewolves do? Healing a little gunshot to the leg should be a breeze."

Damien rolled his eyes. He was losing patience with her outburst.

Faith punched her sister in the shoulder. "What's wrong with you? Why are you being so bitchy?"

She picked up her glass and downed the rest of her Disaronno. "Why don't you ask him?" She hitched her thumb in the direction of Dante.

"That's what this is all about?" Dante's tone sounded razor sharp. Whatever was going on he was on the edge and it showed. "The true mate thing?"

Faith gasped. "You're his mate."

Rebel scoffed, sliding from her stool. "If only he was so lucky. I'm out of here. I've lost interest in anymore of this crap."

"Rebel, wait," Faith called.

She waved her away. "We'll talk tomorrow or maybe the next day. I need a break."

He watched Faith run after her sister, worry etched into her face. "You told her about the true mate thing?"

Dante pushed her hands through his hair and scrubbed his face. "I wanted to be honest with her."

"You know you can still love her without it."

"I know, believe me I know. But if I mate with Rebel and my true mate shows up. I don't know. I just can't do that to her."

"You should go after her. There's nothing Faith can say that will placate her."

Dante nodded. "I will. But first there's something else we need to discuss. We have bigger immediate problems."

Shit. By the look on his brother's face he knew this wasn't going to be good.

"Your rogue wolf escaped."

"What the--how the hell did that happen?"

"That's the really bad part."

Damien glared at him. "Tell me."

"He was snatched by a hunter."

TEN

Faith walked back into the cabin after Dante assured her he would protect her sister. This wolf business was already getting complicated. It seemed surreal that only a couple of days ago she'd taken her final college exams and now she was as far away from that life as she could possibly be. Sometime soon though, they'd have to discuss the fact she still intended to pursue her career. Tacoma was close and it had plenty of opportunity for a new graduate with a forensic science degree. Once she adjusted to her wolf that is.

She found Damien standing at the kitchen bar-- drinking.

Maybe she'd bring it up next week. Or the week after that. For now she had a lot to learn and judging by the scowl on his face, he needed her support. It looked like her dream of spending the next few days in bed with him were about to be crushed.

Still, the compulsion to be near him--touching him consumed her. When she got close, he put down his drink and pulled her into his arms. His familiar heat surrounded her and she inhaled deep drinking in as much of his woodsy male scent as she could get. This evening it seemed stronger, sharper.

"Your sense of smell is heightening, your first shift won't be far behind."

"I'm scared."

He tightened his arms. "Don't be. I'm going to be with you every step of the way."

"What about the rogue? And this hunter thing? Don't you need to be out there hunting or something?" She had no idea of the protocol in situations like this.

"That's the beauty of a pack, no matter how small we are we have each other's back. Diego and Dante will lead the hunt. Your transition is extremely important to the future survival of Devils Point, so you and any other mates will always be the priority."

She wrapped her arms around his waist and held on tight. "What about Rebel?" If they couldn't accept the fact that she needed her twin nearby they were going to have a serious problem.

"True mate or not, Dante's been following her around since the moment she wandered onto our island. I doubt that's going to change."

She wasn't so sure. There was nothing she knew more about her sister than the fact that she would never settle for being second choice.

"Do we have time before my change?"

"Time for what?" he asked, kissing the top of her head.

She lifted her head and found his gaze, licking her lips. "I was thinking maybe you could bite me again."

He growled, a deep rumble that made her heart beat faster.

His nostrils flared at the same time. "Damn. You're already wet."

A huge grin swept across her face. "For a wolf that sure took you long enough."

The smile that he gave her nearly made her panties melt, but when he added a little wolf to the mix with the golden glow around his dilated pupils, she knew she was a goner. He scooped her into his arms and carried her into the bedroom, kicking the door closed behind him.

"Let's hope no one interrupts us this time," she said, laughing.

"If anyone comes through that door unannounced they will do so at their own peril. Nothing--and I mean NOTHING--gets between a shifter and his mate."

He dropped her onto the bed and followed her down, nudging her thighs. "Open," he commanded his handsome face set with a hard, determined look.

In this situation she was more than happy to give him what he wanted.

No sooner did she spread her legs and he was ripping her panties out of the way.

"Hey, I could have just taken those off for you."

"What fun would that have been." He crawled onto the bed and buried his face between her legs.

"Oh my God," she gasped, grabbing onto the sheets. "You could have warned me!"

He rumbled against her sensitive skin and her eyes rolled to the back of her head. Good night this wasn't going to last long at this rate. Already she felt the burn in her belly and the tingle of her spine warning her that an orgasm wouldn't be far behind.

She tried to lift her feet so she could wrap her legs around his back and found them pinned to the bed with hard hands. A sudden thrill shot through her. It had taken her by surprise how much she enjoyed him taking control in the bedroom, now she couldn't get enough. She wanted to stay like this forever.

"Damien," she breathed. His devilish tongue worked expertly as the slow climb to bliss picked up the pace. "You're going to make me come."

Her body jerked and suddenly he no longer had his mouth between her legs.

"Not without me, baby." He kissed his way up her stomach, hitting a particularly sensitive spot that made her knife forward so she got a good look at his mouth and tongue working her. Holy hell he looked like a wild man with his dark hair disheveled, the days old growth of stubble across his chin and cheeks and the taut strain of muscles across his arms and chest.

"Please, don't stop," she begged.

"Mmmm." The sound rumbled across her skin. "It would seem that I have you right where I want you. What will you give me if I keep going?" He kissed a few more inches, bringing his body in alignment to hers. Which meant he was so damned close to being inside her.

"Ugh," she groaned. "You're going to torture me."

"No mate. Not torture. Pleasure." His shaft nudged at her entrance, sliding through the moisture. "What will you give me?"

She tried to wiggle and move so he'd give her more, but she couldn't move. "What do you want? Whatever it is, I'll do it. You're killing me." Her voice trembled.

"It's simple really." He moved another inch forward. "I want your wolf, baby."

"Don't you already have it? You bit me." He smiled, the devilish grin that nearly broke her heart with want.

"I need to see her."

She held his gaze and watched as his eyes darkened a moment before the golden glow of the wolf looked down on her.

"Let me see her."

Something stirred inside Faith. It was so deep she couldn't imagine where it came from, but she recognized that he was coaxing it out of her.

"Holy shit, baby. She's so beautiful."

His words were killing her. She imagined him seeing what she saw. The beautiful, caring man with the wild wolf straining inside him. Right then her skin felt like it was going to burst. She felt the blood moving under her skin. More of her lived than ever before.

"What's happening?"

"Your wolf is being born and she is going to be magnificent. Not to mention all mine."

A wave of possession washed over her with a clarity that shocked the hell out of her. "You belong to me too, Damien."

"Damn fucking right. Now take it."

She lifted again and grabbed his face, never tearing her gaze from his. "If you don't fuck me right this instant I am going to die from this ache and then I'll haunt your ass for eternity. Is that what you want?"

"Eternity yes, dying hell no." He shoved his face in her neck and surged forward.

She screamed at the sudden move as her orgasm hit, sending shards of pleasure to every point of her body.

Damien lifted his head and howled and began to move, fucking her hard. His gaze held her captive and she watched the man/wolf the whole time. Warm breath and soft gasps filled the room. She was lost and found all at the same time.

So close. Her eyes fluttered closed as the precipice called to her.

"Keep them open, Faith. Look at me when you come."

That did it. Holy hell. It shot through her forcing a scream from her throat. His face darkened, a deeper hunger than before consuming him. He pushed forward and groaned deep, never taking his eyes from hers.

"Mine."

"Hell yes," she said. "All yours and all mine."

Thank you so much for reading!

READY TO CONTINUE with more Devils Point Wolves? Dante and Rebel are going to get downright wicked!

One click **WICKED** which is available now.

If you enjoyed this story please take a moment to help other readers discover it by leaving a review on your favorite retailer.

Just a few words and some stars really does help!

Join Eliza's VIP newsletter at elizagayle.com/newsletter and be the first to be notified of new releases, sales and contests.

If you're on Facebook or Tiktok, come by and say hello! I'd love to hear from you.

Continue reading for a sneak peek from Wicked, the next book in the Devils Point Wolves series and the full booklist from Eliza Gayle.

SNEAK PEEK FROM WICKED

WICKED

By Eliza Gayle

Copyright 2015

All Rights Reserved

Book Description:

What do you do when the woman he wants more than anything else isn't his true mate...Brace yourself.

Rebel has one last thing to do before she can walk away from her life on Devils Point and the man she can't get out of her head.

Find the shifter who hurt her sister.

She'll have to work with Dante to make it happen and that might be the final straw that breaks her. Unless she can come up with an idea to get him out of her system.

Like one night of no holds barred sex. Hot, dirty and thoroughly... Yeah, she definitely needs to get her mind out of the gutter.

Dante thought he was waiting for his mate. It's what they were taught and what every wolf yearns for. But this mating season brought him a different kind of woman.

Curvy, feisty and downright wicked.

She is also not his true mate and everyone thinks he should let her go. Too bad she's under his skin and he doesn't know what to do about it.

Well...he actually does have some ideas about that.

BONUS CHAPTER - WICKED

Dante repeated the name in his head as soon as the host announced the next dancer to hit the stage at Club Diablo, all while contemplating the ways he could make her pay.

Rebel.

She strutted on stage and he got lost in the sight of her. Leather vest over a leather micro mini skirt, boots up to her thighs, all revealing the creamy flesh he couldn't keep his hands off no matter how hard he tried.

She'd changed her hair from its original frothy blonde color to a fire engine red. It did not change the level of magnetism he felt looking at her. In fact it might have made it worse. Red drew the eye and it caught his attention as he watched it cascade down her back and skim the top of her ass. Did he mention what a fantastic ass she had? Dante swallowed a groan. He already knew what it felt like to have his hands cupped around those perfect cheeks and he wanted it again. She might be the twin to his brother's mate, Faith, but in his mind they looked nothing alike.

They were night and day. Light and dark. Wicked and sweet.

His body tightened the more he thought of her until his pants grew uncomfortable and he wanted to drive into something. Preferably her. Except for the past two weeks she'd kept her distance. Not an actual physical distance since they'd spent a lot of time together trying to find the rogue wolf that bit her sister and the possible hunter that he was beginning to believe might have been a figment of his imagination. How else did he explain no sign of him for two weeks? People disappeared all the time, but Dante wasn't human and it wasn't easy for a human to disappear from a wolf without a trace. Every human carried a unique scent that allowed them to be easily tracked.

Rebel reached for the pole and the thoughts of hunters and rogues disappeared from his mind. Her hips rotated, making him think of sex again. Every thrust and grind as she whipped around the stage like it was nothing drove him higher. How many times had he seen her dance now? He'd lost track. But every time was like the first time as he began silently chanting in his head for her to take off her clothes.

The men around the stage were crowding closer as they usually did. She was one of their most popular dancers. Hard not to be when she represented everything that one might dream a bad girl would be like. Beyond the new fiery hair and the tight leather clothes, Rebel had an air about her that anyone could guess came with a pretty big bite.

Maybe it was the tattoos that adorned parts of her. He'd never seen that much ink on a woman, but damn did it turn him on.

Apparently, whenever she traveled to a new place she liked to take home a permanent souvenir. He'd already memorized them all, but had yet to learn the story behind everyone one. He did know the sugar skull on her back was from a wild weekend in Mexico with some people she barely knew. And the wine bottle wrapped in thorns came from a month in California wine country with some rich guy that she claimed had a fetish for bad girls.

That was another thing about Rebel. She attracted everyone and made friends with nearly all of them. And yet somehow managed to never let anyone get too close. Even her sister was forced to remain in her life from a distance.

Apparently Rebel didn't carry the twin gene that made them want to be connected at all times. Although he was pretty sure Faith did. It didn't take a genius to pick up the little nuances of the newest member of their pack. Whenever she spent time with Rebel her eyes filled with a sadness that pulled at everyone around her. She didn't think anyone noticed, but he did and so did Rebel.

Whatever was going on inside that women, she didn't like disappointing her sister. The loss of their parents a few years back had created some sort of rift between them and so far neither seemed to know how to fix it. Dante knew this because Damien was on a tear about trying to help them deal with it. His brother was a little nuts about doing whatever it took to make his new mate happy.

Pussy.

The thought of Damien convincing Rebel to do anything made Dante laugh. He couldn't imagine her welcoming any interference from his brother. She was still pissed at all of them. Two weeks back she'd walked into a fight between he and Damien that had resulted in him going wolf and scaring the hell out of her.

Not exactly how he'd wanted her to find out.

Rebel peeled her leather vest off and revealed generous breasts that were now bare except for the red pasties covering her nipples. His mouth watered. Rebel wasn't like most humans when it came to her body. She wasn't afraid to reveal it in any way and she seemed to revel in showing it off. Although when he asked her about it she said it was all about the money.

Club Diablo paid their dancers very well. As the main business that brought income to the island, it was important to them all to make sure the guests who came in were treated extremely well. By paying the dancers over the norm they not only got the best talent, they didn't have a lot of turnover, which suited them perfectly. Although it wasn't easy to find strippers that appealed to shifters. They were aggressive and interested in women who were not stick thin. It took a little meat on the bones to handle sex with a wolf.

So they paid extra to find them.

Living on an island might make their pack feel isolated, in reality they weren't. They were surrounded on three sides by a peninsula with a variety of small towns from tiny to average. And with Tacoma so close, Washington didn't feel quite as big as it used to. In fact, with a hunter possibly wandering their lands and a rogue loose at the same time, the real world encroached far more than was comfortable.

Dante scanned the faces in the crowd watching Rebel's performance, looking for a hint of either the hunter or the rogue. All they had to go on was a description of the rogue in wolf form and the scent of the hunter that had more to do with their weapons than the actual person. His pack hated guns and their scent that permeated everything.

He stilled on one quickly becoming familiar face. He didn't know the man but he recognized him as a repeat customer. Dante took a slow deep breath and filtered through the scents of the room. Not an easy feat with this many people this close and in an aroused state.

Above it all he scented Rebel though. A heady fragrance of jasmine from the lotion she kept in her purse and reapplied often, to the light sheen of sweat that made her body glisten under the lights. She was up on the pole now working it with the strong muscles of her inner thighs. He could easily imagine those long legs of hers wrapped around his waist as he drove into her. He ground his teeth to force down the growl that threatened. Watching her was easy enough, but knowing what went through the minds of the other men as they watched her wasn't. They wanted to fuck her too.

Dante sighed. This is why he and his brothers did not get involved with the dancers if they could help it. Mixing business with pleasure led to disastrous results. His brother, Diego had learned that the hard way when a human dancer wormed her way under his skin and then...

A sharp scent filtered through his scents and Dante jerked his head in the direction. A strong odor of metal. It disappeared as quickly as he scented it. He searched the room for the source. Was the hunter right here under his own nose? He growled, not bothering to hide it. A few of the shifter customers turned their heads and looked.

Either not interested in his business or reluctant to get involved, they all slowly turned back to the show when they realized he stood nearby. As long as they weren't who he hunted, they had nothing to fear. He had no plans to screw up the good thing they had going here with Club Diablo. This establishment easily funded ninety percent of the island's operation, making it easier for the pack to keep to themselves instead of seeking employment off island.

There were other establishments that contributed to the welfare of the pack like the diner and motel but nothing compared to the Diablo. In recent years a few of the pack members had expressed concern about their sole source of income and initiatives had begun for other avenues of revenue. Some old school and some not. They even had a dot com style start up that some of the pups were working on getting off the ground. Whatever they did was over his head. Other than the things they did online to market Club Diablo, he didn't have much use for technology other than the cell phone he carried around to keep in touch.

Some new catcalls from the stage area again caught his attention and he turned around just in time to see Rebel removing her skirt and throwing it above her head.

His mouth went dry. Like the pasties, the thong she wore was as red as her hair and the gloss she wore on her lips.

Fuck. He wanted to bite that scrap of silk off of her and bury his face between her thighs. They'd gone out a few times after hours as friends and each time things got a little more heated than he'd planned. Hard to stay in control when she seemed as eager as him to engage in some hot fucking sex.

He closed his eyes and reached deep for some shred of sanity that would keep him in place and not stalking to the stage and throwing her over his shoulder and taking her home.

That's what was killing him. This fucking mating season. That had to be why he couldn't stop thinking of laying hands on her. She'd made it perfectly clear she didn't want him anywhere near her anymore.

Unfortunately, everything that came out of her mouth these days filled him with rage. Like her half-baked plan to serve as bait for the rogue that bit her sister. He still couldn't believe that his pack agreed with her. Or that his brothers also went along with the idea. Bastards.

As if she could hear his thoughts she turned her gaze to his on cue, giving him a look that clearly said fuck you. He clenched his jaw.

"You are a glutton for punishment." His brother Diego walked up next to him, a half smile across his face.

"You think that's funny?"

"Fuck yeah. She makes you squirm and that is a sight to behold."

Dante growled again. "You're supposed to be helping me find our rogue in the crowd not waste time giving me shit."

"I am an excellent multitasker."

It was then he noticed his brother's tight body language. To the casual observer he looked like nothing more than a man enjoying the show, but to him the subtle nuances such as the hard set of his jaw told Dante he was anything but a relaxed onlooker.

"Where's Damien?" he asked.

"Where do you think?" Diego smirked.

Dante sighed. Since turning his new mate wolf two weeks ago, they'd spent every waking moment running or fucking. He loved his brother and was happy he'd reconciled with his true mate, but this was mating season and it was driving them all a little crazier than usual it seemed.

"Any sign of our guy?"

Diego nodded his head. "Just that one dude to the right of the stage sitting in the shadows. His attention is fixated on Rebel, but he looks nervous. He fidgets a lot."

His brother had pointed out the same man he suspected, except he'd missed the nervous tics Diego easily discovered.

"We really going to do this? Just let her walk out of here unprotected?" he asked.

Diego shook his head. "She won't exactly be unprotected. Someone will have eyes on her the whole way."

"It only takes a second for this asshole to bite her or worse. Not even the fastest wolf in our pack will be able to stop that." And the thought of someone hurting her made him angry. A festering wound kind of anger that never relented.

"She's not exactly a pushover, dude."

"No match for a wolf."

Diego scoffed. "She has no problem taking you down."

"That's different." She'd grabbed his crotch and tried to neuter him. "She may not look like it on the outside, but she's vulnerable. And this is a bad idea."

Diego turned to him. "She made up her mind and she's determined. I agree that it's a dangerous thing for a human to take on. But I get why she needs to do it. You know as well as I do that you have to let her do this. Otherwise, she'll never trust the pack and you know we can't live with that."

Dante tried to ignore his brother's logic, but it was impossible. Without trust she'd have difficulty keeping their secrets. This wasn't what he hoped for her. He thought when she found out about his kind she'd be more on board. Everything he'd seen and learned about her said she had a very open mind.

"No, we can't have that," he admitted. There was no greater priority than keeping their existence a secret. Especially now that extremists with more hate than logic, were turning hunters more and more these days.

"Any sign of the hunter?"

Diego shook his head.

"Someone took a shot at the wolf in front of Faith. And that bullet casing I found smelled like silver. Hunter or not someone knows something and they could fuck one of us up if they're screwing around."

Dante turned his attention back to the stage when he realized Rebel's music was beginning to fade. The fake smoke filled the front and all he saw was the swing of her wicked red hair and the sway of bare hips...

Diego walked closer and nudged his side. "Time to take our places, bro. Don't worry. She's going to be fine."

Dante frowned. "Isn't there a stupid saying about famous last words?"

Available now

ALSO BY ELIZA GAYLE

Southern Shifters: Dragon Kings Trilogy:

THE CURSE OF THE DRAGON

THE SOUL OF THE DRAGON

THE FIRE OF THE DRAGON

Southern Shifters:

SHIFTER MARKED

MATE NIGHT

ALPHA KNOWS BEST

BAD KITTY

BE WERE

SHIFTIN' DIRTY

BEAR NAKED TRUTH

ALPHA BEAST

ONE CRAZY WOLF

Enigma Shifters Fated Mates:

DRAGON MATED

WOLF BAITED

BEARLY DATED

WOLF TEMPTED

Devils Point Wolves:

WILD

WICKED

WANTED

FERAL

FIERCE

FURY

Single titles:

VAMPIRE AWAKENING

WITCH AND WERE

GABE'S OBSESSION

GABE'S RECKONING

Purgatory Club:

ROPED

WATCH ME

TEASED

BURN

BOTTOMS UP

HOLD ME CLOSE

Pleasure Playground Series:

PLAY WITH ME

POWER PLAY

Single Title:

TAMING BEAUTY

WICKED CHRISTMAS EVE

Gypsy Ink Books
www.gypsyinkbooks.wordpress.com